Piggy and Dad Go Fishing

David Martin   illustrated by Frank Remkiewicz

SCHOLASTIC INC.
New York   Toronto   London   Auckland   Sydney
Mexico City   New Delhi   Hong Kong   Buenos Aires

Piggy and Dad Go Fishing

For Luna and Rory and their dads
D. M.

For Dick Shute
F. R.

ISBN-13: 978-0-545-03012-0
ISBN-10: 0-545-03012-9

Text copyright © 2005 by David Martin.
Illustrations copyright © 2005 by Frank Remkiewicz.
All rights reserved. Published by Scholastic Inc., 557 Broadway,
New York, NY 10012, by arrangement with Candlewick Press.
SCHOLASTIC and associated logos are trademarks
and/or registered trademarks of Scholastic Inc.

12 11 10 9 8 7 6 5 4 3 2 1   7 8 9 10 11/0

Printed in the U.S.A.   40

This edition first printing, March 2007

This book was typeset in Kosmik.

The illustrations were done in watercolor and pencil.

Piggy woke up excited.

Today he was going fishing with Dad for the very first time.

Dad was already up getting the fishing poles ready and making Piggy's favorite lunch—peanut butter and jelly sandwiches on squishy bread.

"Now all we need are worms, and tonight we'll have the world's most delicious fried fresh fish for supper," said Dad.

So Piggy dug up worms faster than he could say *delicious fried fresh fish.*

When they got to the river, Dad asked Piggy if he wanted to bait his own hook.

"Okay," said Piggy. He took a worm and hung it over his hook.

The worm wiggled and fell off.

Piggy tried again.
This time he tied the worm in a knot around the hook.

The worm untied itself.

"Piggy, I'm afraid you really have to poke the hook into the worm."

Piggy looked at the worm. The worm smiled at Piggy.

"Do you want me to do it?" Dad asked.

Dad looked at the worm.

The worm smiled at Dad.

"Let's use bread for bait instead," said Dad.

So Piggy and Dad pinched bread from their sandwiches, squished it into little balls, and baited their hooks.

Then they threw in their lines.

"Now," said Dad as he sat down, "you have to be very patient. Fishing takes a lot of waiting. A fish has to be hungry. It has to think about eating. It has to find the bait. It has to look at the bait and think about it and say to itself, *That looks pretty tasty*. It has to nibble the bait and decide if it really is good. And then, finally, it has to bite the whole thing, hook and all."

But Piggy wasn't good at waiting.

He pulled his line out

and threw it back in

and pulled it out

and threw it back in again and again.

"Nothing's happening," he said.

"You can't hurry fish," said Dad.

Soon they both fell asleep.

But they held on to their poles.

Suddenly Piggy's pole bent hard.
"I got a bite!" he shouted.
Piggy pulled. The fish pulled.
Piggy pulled again, and the fish
pulled again too. The fish jumped.

Piggy slipped.

Dad grabbed Piggy.
Dad slipped.

splash!

But finally Piggy reeled in his fish.

"Good job," said Dad.
"It's a beauty."

Piggy smiled. But then he looked at his fish, and his fish was looking right back at him.

"My fish looks sad," said Piggy.

"Do you think he really feels sad?"

"I don't know. I never thought about it," said Dad.

Piggy and the fish stared at each other.

"Can I let him go?" said Piggy.

"Sure," said Dad. So Piggy slipped the fish back into the water.

"Bye-bye, fishie," said Piggy. "Watch out for hooks next time."

The fish flipped its tail and was gone.

Then, while they ate lunch, Piggy made more bread balls and tossed them into the water.

"What are you doing?" asked Dad.

"I'm fishing," said Piggy.

"But you're just feeding the fish," said Dad.

"I know. That's because it's a different kind of fishing. You should try it," said Piggy.

"Look at all the fish!" said Dad. "This is fun. Why didn't I ever think of feed-the-fish fishing?"

The next day, Piggy and Dad went fishing again. As a special treat, Dad brought doughnuts. Some for Piggy, some for himself, and all the rest for the fish.

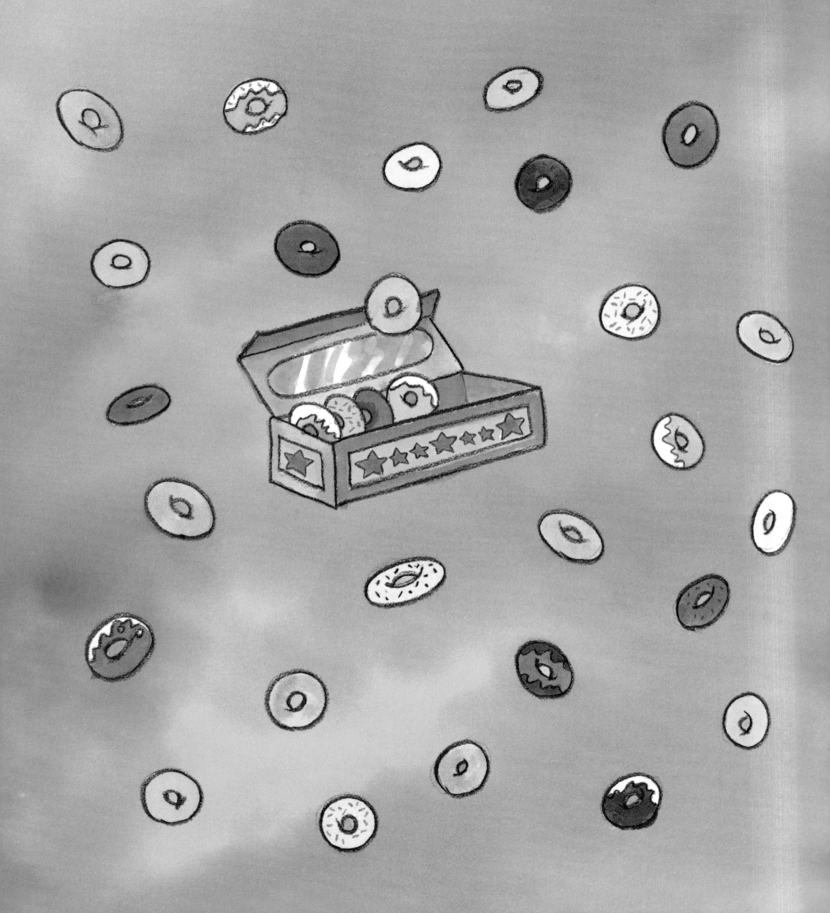

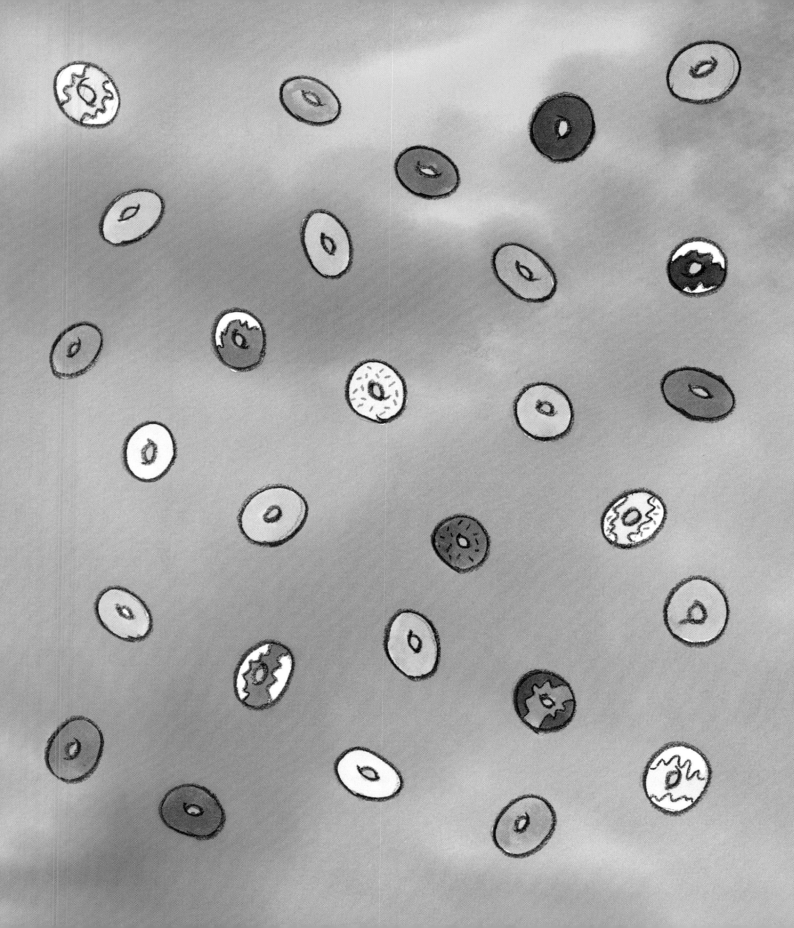